CONCORD CUNNINGHAM
THE

By
Mathew Halverson

Concord Cunningham:
The *Scripture Sleuth*
Mathew Halverson

Copyright © 2000 FOCUS PUBLISHING
All rights reserved.

No part of this book may be reproduced by any means without written consent of the publisher except for brief quotes used in reviews written specifically for use in a magazine or newspaper.

Cover Illustration by Don Stewart
Cover Design by Richard Schaefer

ISBN 1-885904-19-3

PRINTED IN THE UNITED STATES OF AMERICA
by
FOCUS PUBLISHING
Bemidji, Minnesota 56601

For Lori and Emma

Contents

1
THE VASE CASE

Before yesterday, people in the northwestern town of Pine Tops didn't know what a Scripture Sleuth was. They knew that the word "Scripture" meant the Bible. They knew that a sleuth solved mysteries like a detective. But they didn't understand how somebody could use the Bible to solve everyday mysteries.

It made perfect sense to Concord Cunningham. No matter what the mystery was, he could find a clue in the Bible to help solve it.

Unfortunately, he could also find the canned spinach in the local grocery store.

"Maybe it'll be sold out, Concord," his dad said as they walked down the vegetable aisle. "We can only hope," Concord said with a sigh. He dreaded the spinach casserole his mom was making for dinner.

A few steps later, Concord's expression fell as he saw that the spinach shelf was fully stocked. But he wasn't ready to admit defeat. He spent two whole minutes making sure he had selected the tiniest can available. Just as he was putting the can into the grocery cart, his dad's cellular phone rang.

"It's probably the paper," Mr. Cunningham said, reaching into his overcoat pocket for the phone. As the top reporter for the *Ponderosa Press*, the local newspaper, Mr. Cunningham was always called when there was a breaking story.

"Hello," the tall reporter answered. He listened for a

moment, then pulled out his notepad and began scribbling. "I see. What was stolen? Okay," he said as he looked at his watch. "I'll get over there right away."

Mr. Cunningham put the phone back into his coat pocket and turned to Concord. "We've got a change of plans, Concord. How would you like to help me cover a story?"

"You bet," Concord said excitedly. He'd always wanted to go with his dad on a reporting assignment. "What's the story?"

"An antique vase was stolen from the Blue Spruce Apartments this morning," Mr. Cunningham said. "We need to get to the crime scene right away. My editor wants to put the story in the evening edition of the newspaper."

"I guess the spinach casserole will have to wait," Concord said with a grin, putting the tiny can of spinach back onto the shelf.

"No complaints here," Mr. Cunningham said, grinning back. "I'm sure your mom will understand."

They hurried out of the store and quickly drove across town. They were soon parked along the curb in front of the Blue Spruce apartment building. As they got out of the car, Concord grabbed his backpack and slung it over his shoulder. He seldom went anywhere without it.

The Cunninghams entered the building, and an elderly doorman greeted them suspiciously in the lobby. Mr. Cunningham fumbled through his pockets and finally found his press pass. He held it out for the doorman to see.

The doorman glanced at the pass and then looked back at Mr. Cunningham. "The police are up on the seventh floor," he said. "That's where it happened."

"Okay. And which apartment?" Mr. Cunningham asked.

"There's only one apartment on the seventh floor, the penthouse. That's the top of the building," the doorman said. "The stairs are right over there."

"What about the elevator?" Concord asked, glancing across the lobby.

"It hasn't worked for months," the doorman grumbled.

"Thanks for your help," Mr. Cunningham said cheerfully. He and Concord headed for the stairs.

When they emerged on the seventh floor, Police Chief Riggins motioned Mr. Cunningham into the large apartment.

Chief Riggins was a plump man with a neatly trimmed mustache, and he always wore a freshly pressed uniform. He and Mr. Cunningham knew each other well from past crimes that Mr. Cunningham had reported.

"Just a minute, Bill," Chief Riggins said, holding up his hand. "Who's your new partner?"

"Oh, this is my son, Concord," he replied. "He'll stay out of the way."

The chief rubbed his chin and looked down at the slim, sandy-haired boy.

"I guess it's all right," he decided. "Just don't touch anything, Conrad."

"That's Concord," Concord corrected.

"Uh, right," the chief mumbled.

"So what have you got so far, Chief?" Mr. Cunningham asked as he pulled out his reporter's notebook.

"Well," Chief Riggins began, "the vase was stolen while the tenant, Mrs. Jessen, was out running errands this morning. We think the thief is sitting right over there." Concord and his dad looked across the room. Sitting on the couch was a man wearing jeans, a T-shirt, and a tool belt. "He's an electrician who's been working in the building today," Chief Riggins continued. "We found the stolen vase in his van, which is parked down in the alley."

"That was a pretty quick investigation," said Mr. Cunningham.

"Yeah, except it isn't quite over," the chief said. "The electrician says he didn't steal the vase. He says somebody else stole it and put it in his van."

"And you believe him?" Mr. Cunningham asked with surprise.

"Normally, we probably wouldn't," the chief admitted, "but we can't figure out how the electrician could possibly be the thief."

Mr. Cunningham stopped writing and looked up at the chief. "What do you mean?" he asked.

"Well, did you two notice anything special in the stairwell when you climbed up here?" the chief asked.

Concord nodded. "There were security cameras," he said.

Mr. Cunningham looked down at Concord, impressed with the observation.

Chief Riggins grinned. "Very good, Conway."

"That's Concord," Concord corrected.

"Uh, right," the chief mumbled. "Anyway, we've looked at the recording that the security cameras made. The tape shows that the electrician made two trips up the stairs to the seventh floor while Mrs. Jessen was gone. But, the tape also shows that the electrician was not carrying a single thing on either of those trips. Not the vase, not something that he could hide the vase in or under, not anything."

"And nobody else came up to the seventh floor while Mrs. Jessen was gone?" Mr. Cunningham asked.

"Not according to the security tape," the chief said.

"And we don't think there's any way up here without being seen by those cameras."

"Could somebody have climbed up the outside of the building and come in a window?" Mr. Cunningham asked.

The chief shook his head. He walked over to the window and looked down at the alley. "Mrs. Jessen said that she always keeps the windows closed and locked. She also said that all the windows were still locked from the inside when she got home, and none of them were broken."

"What about the possibility of somebody climbing up the elevator shaft?" Concord asked.

"The security cameras also monitor every opening to the elevator shaft, even though the elevator hasn't been working for a while," the chief said. "The tape shows that nobody has been in the elevator shaft today."

"Sounds like you've got your work cut out for you, Chief," Mr. Cunningham said. He started looking back through his notes to see if he had missed anything. "Oh, I almost forgot. Did Mrs. Jessen report anything else stolen?" Mr. Cunningham asked.

"She didn't report anything else stolen, and we didn't find anything else in the electrician's van. But Mrs. Jessen did report a couple other strange things," the chief said as his forehead wrinkled. "She said that she had a picnic basket all packed for lunch in Evergreen Park this afternoon. When she got back from her errands, all the food had been taken out of it."

"So the thief was hungry?" Concord asked.

"That's what I thought, too" Chief Riggins chuckled, giving Concord a soft slap on the back. "But all the picnic food was just sitting on the kitchen table. Not one piece of it was eaten."

Concord's eyes began to dart back and forth. The situation was reminding him of something he had read in the Bible.

"Was there anything else strange?" Concord asked.

"One other thing," said Chief Riggins. "Mrs. Jessen said that it looked like somebody took a nap in her bed. All the blankets were messed up. She says that whoever napped there must have been pretty cold, too, because every extra blanket from her closet was also on the bed."

Concord nodded as he thought about the clues. Then he opened his backpack and pulled out his Bible. He turned to a chapter in the book of Acts and began reading. A moment later, Concord's eyes locked on a verse, and a grin moved across his face.

"Chief, the electrician did steal the vase and put it in the van," Concord announced, "and he did it all by himself."

The entire room fell silent. The electrician raised one of his eyebrows and looked over at Concord from the couch. The chief bent down and flashed a quick grin at Concord.

"How could he possibly do that?" the chief asked doubtfully.

"The proof is right here in Acts 9:25," Concord said.

The electrician laughed and looked relieved.

The chief stood up with a look of confusion. "Acts 9:25?" he questioned, looking at Concord like he was crazy. "In the Bible?"

"That's right!" Concord exclaimed.

Curiosity got the best of the chief, so he bent down to read Concord's Bible. After a moment he looked up, winked at Concord, and then arrested the electrician for the theft of Mrs. Jessen's vase.

How did the electrician steal the vase?

Read Acts 9:25 to find the clue that Chief Riggins got from Concord.

The solution to *"The Vase Case"* is on page 80.

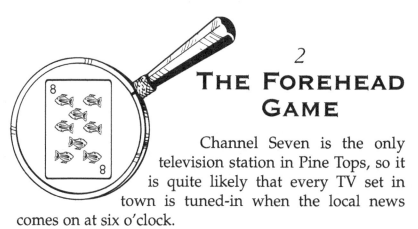

2
THE FOREHEAD
GAME

Channel Seven is the only television station in Pine Tops, so it is quite likely that every TV set in town is tuned-in when the local news comes on at six o'clock.

That night, at 6:01 p.m., every jaw in Pine Tops dropped when Police Chief Riggins credited Concord for solving the Blue Spruce Apartments theft. At 6:02 P.M., every eye opened wide when Chief Riggins explained how the Scripture Sleuth had used a Bible passage to solve the crime. Then, half of Pine Tops chuckled with approval as the chief referred to Concord as "The Concordance." Meanwhile, the other half scrambled for dictionaries to look up the definition for "concordance." They, too, chuckled at the nickname when they discovered that a concordance tells readers where to find certain words and passages in the Bible.

Later that evening, Concord went downstairs and found his older brother, Cody, playing cards with three friends. Just as Concord, Cody had been named after a town that Mr. and Mrs. Cunningham had lived in before they moved to Pine Tops.

Cody was a few inches taller than Concord, and he had short, curly brown hair.

"Hey, there's Pine Tops' newest crime buster!" cried one of Cody's friends.

"Way to go, little bro'!" exclaimed Cody as he gave Concord a high-five.

"Thanks," Concord said with a grin. "Can I play?"

"Sorry, Concord," Cody said. "Older kids only. You can watch for a while if you want."

Concord accepted the offer and sat down next to his brother.

It was a strange game. Each player was dealt one card, face-down. Without looking at the card, each player lifted the card and pressed it to his forehead so the rest of the group could see what it was. Each player then knew what every other player had, but he didn't know what card was displayed on his own forehead.

Each player would then guess if his own card was the highest, the second highest, the third highest, or the lowest of the group. Since it was impossible to know for sure, there was a significant amount of luck involved.

"Dustin is unbelievable," Cody said. "His last fourteen guesses have been correct! He says he's psychic," Cody said suspiciously.

"I've always thought I have superior mental powers," Dustin boasted.

Everyone groaned as the chubby redhead smirked.

It was Cody's turn to deal, so he grabbed the deck and began shuffling the cards. He decided to shuffle twice as long as usual. He wanted to make sure that Dustin had no clue to the order of the cards. Dustin didn't seem at all concerned.

Cody was just about to deal when Mrs. Cunningham walked in.

"More root beer anyone?" she offered.

"No thanks," a couple of them mumbled, having already consumed three root beers apiece.

"Since you're offering, I'll take a glass of lemonade," Concord said.

"I think I can manage a glass of lemonade for The

Concordance," Mrs. Cunningham said with a smile. "Dustin, would you like a refill on your water?" she asked.

"No thank you, Mrs. Cunningham, I've got plenty," he said as he lifted his green mug and took a sip. "Ah, good stuff. I'll bet it's what keeps my psychic powers fresh."

"Sooner or later, your so-called psychic powers are going to reach their expiration date," Cody joked as he dealt the cards. The group laughed, and Mrs. Cunningham chuckled under her breath as she left to get Concord's drink.

Each player took his card and held it up to his own forehead, face-out. Concord, and everyone else, studied Dustin closely when he moved his card from the table to his forehead. The group agreed that Dustin had no chance to sneak a peak at the face of his card. He didn't even appear to try.

The four players then looked at the cards on each other's foreheads. After a moment of thought, Cody made his guess. The other two boys eventually made their guesses, leaving only Dustin to guess. He slowly studied the cards on the other three foreheads and then began to rub his temple with his free hand.

He said in a quiet voice, "It's coming to me. It's coming to me."

The group groaned. Dustin lifted his head and stared at the ceiling. Then he looked down at the table in deep concentration. Then he looked at each forehead again.

"Ah, yes. I can sense it!" he exclaimed. "My card is the third highest."

They all peeled the cards off their foreheads and placed them face-up on the table. Cody had a five, Dustin had an eight, and the other two boys had a nine and a ten. Dustin's card was third highest, just as he had predicted. He was right for the fifteenth time in a row! Cody and the other two boys shook their heads in disgust.

As the next player grabbed the deck and dealt another hand, Concord scratched his cheek with curiosity. He walked over to a bookshelf and scanned the books. Finding a Bible, he pulled it off the shelf and opened it. This Bible had a concordance section in the back. Concord turned to it, and he began looking through the different subjects that were listed. He finally found the word he was looking for: "water." Below the word "water" was a list of Bible verses, and Concord started looking them up.

Soon Concord heard the players groan. Dustin had done it again.

Dustin looked over at Concord. "So, Concord, have you ever met a psychic before?" he asked boastfully.

"Nope," Concord replied as he scanned a page in Proverbs. Then his finger stopped on a verse, and he looked up with a grin. "And I still haven't."

"What?" Dustin said, surprised that Concord wasn't impressed.

"Your psychic abilities are fake," Concord said confidently. "Proverbs 27:19 explains it all."

The four boys looked at each other.

Concord walked over to the table and placed the open Bible in front of them. After reading Proverbs 27:19, Cody proclaimed, "The Concordance has struck again! Dustin, you're busted!"

How did Dustin always know what to guess?

Read Proverbs 27:19 to find the clue that Concord gave the guys.

The solution to *"The Forehead Game"* is on page 81.

3
SIDEWALK
CHALK TALK

Pine Tops pedestrians are always glancing down when they walk past Leonard Mincy's house. They aren't trying to avoid Leonard or his parents. They just can't keep their eyes off the sidewalk.

Leonard sketches beautiful colored chalk drawings on the sidewalk in front of his house. People are always excited to see what Leonard's newest creation is. Sometimes they walk blocks out of their way just to enjoy what has become known as the "sidewalk gallery."

Concord was looking forward to walking past the sidewalk gallery after today's soccer practice. He hadn't been in that neighborhood in a couple weeks, and he was excited to see what Leonard had been drawing.

As Concord walked up to Leonard's latest sidewalk sketch, he decided to pause for a moment to appreciate it. After tilting his head to the left and then to the right, Concord decided he had to be looking at the drawing upside down. He walked to the other side and tilted his head to the left, then to the right, but he was still puzzled.

Finally, Concord realized that the sketch was only half-done. He wasn't sure, but it looked to him as if the finished drawing was going to be a dog eating a fire hydrant. He was amused as he imagined the silly scene.

Anxious to see the other drawings, Concord resumed his walk along the sidewalk gallery. He had only gone a few feet when he realized that Leonard was sitting on the curb just down the street. Leonard's chin was cupped in his hands.

"Taking a break, Leonard?" Concord called down the sidewalk.

"Worse," Leonard replied with a sigh. "The Burley twins stole my chalk."

"They didn't even let you finish your drawing of the dog eating the fire hydrant?" Concord asked.

"The what?" Leonard asked as he adjusted his glasses on his nose.

"You know, your newest . . . drawing," Concord explained, suddenly realizing his guess must be totally wrong.

"Oh. Well, uh, that's going to be a rhinoceros," Leonard said. "But, yeah, that's why it isn't finished. I went inside for a minute to get a snack. When I came back out, my chalk was gone. I looked down the street and saw the Burley twins running toward the town square. I would have gone after them, but I figured two Burley twins against one Leonard Mincy wasn't a very good situation."

"Yeah, I don't blame you," Concord agreed. He dropped his backpack on the curb and sat down next to Leonard.

An idea sparked in Leonard's mind. "Hey, I heard that you proved some criminal was guilty by using the Bible. Does the Bible work with chalk thefts?" he asked.

"I've never met a situation the Bible can't solve," Concord replied. "And I sure would like to see the other half of that dog eating the—I mean, the other half of the rhinoceros," he added with a smile.

Leonard jumped to his feet. "Then let's go to the town square," he said. Concord agreed, and they were off.

The town square was a large courtyard in downtown Pine Tops. It was bordered by tall evergreen trees, various shops, and friendly cafes. At one end of the courtyard was a large fountain. At the other end stood a tall statue of an old lumberjack swinging a big axe. It was dedicated to the loggers who had founded Pine Tops back in the late 1800's.

When Concord and Leonard arrived, Bart and Bernie Burley were sitting underneath the lumberjack statue. The two muscular, blond boys were admiring the chalk drawing they had made on the cement courtyard beneath the statue. When Bart Burley saw Leonard and Concord approaching, he slapped Bernie's arm.

"Look, Leonard decided to bring The Concordance to see how real artists draw," Bart said with a laugh.

Concord decided not to waste any time. "Hi guys. Leonard says that the chalk you're using is his," he stated.

"No way," Bart moaned. "This chalk is ours. We've had it for a long time."

"More like twenty minutes!" Leonard cried. "That's when you stole it off my sidewalk. I saw you running off with it!"

"Did not!" shouted Bernie. "We've been drawing with this chalk all morning."

"Okay, okay," Concord said to the group, trying to calm everyone down. He turned to the twins. "Can you prove that you've had the chalk longer than twenty minutes?" he asked.

The twins huddled. Bart whispered something into Bernie's ear. Then Bernie shook his head and whispered something into Bart's ear. Bart nodded, and they broke their huddle.

"You want proof? Look at this drawing on the concrete," Bart said smugly.

Concord and Leonard looked down and saw a chalk drawing of the lumberjack statue that was standing above them.

"It's the lumberjack," Concord stated.

"Very good, Mr. Concordance," snapped Bernie. "We traced the shadow of the statue on the concrete."

Concord and Leonard looked up and saw the sky filled with clouds. The sun couldn't be seen anywhere.

"Ha!" Leonard said as he put his hands on his hips. "It's totally cloudy. You can't trace a shadow if the sun isn't out."

"Thank you for proving our point, Leonard," Bart boasted. "It's cloudy now, which means we couldn't have traced the shadow in the last twenty minutes."

Leonard's smile changed to a frown. He had fallen right into their trap. It was true, the sun hadn't been shining for the last twenty minutes, but it had been out earlier in the day.

Concord knelt down to take a closer look at the drawing.

"No offense," Concord said, "but for tracing something, you sure didn't do a very good job. The lines are shaky. You could have just drawn this on your own, without a shadow to guide you."

The twins turned back into a huddle. Bart whispered to Bernie. Then Bernie whispered to Bart. Then they turned back to Concord.

"No offense taken," Bart said. "The lines are shaky because we're both right-handed."

"What does that have to do with it?" Leonard asked.

"We traced the shadow with our left hands," Bernie replied. "That's why the lines are so shaky. And we trace much slower with our left hands. That's why it took us two hours to trace it. You see, just as we told you, we've had the chalk all morning." The twins exchanged a high-five.

Leonard looked to Concord. "I guess it's my word against theirs, Concord," he said.

"Not necessarily," Concord replied. He opened up his

backpack and pulled out his Bible. As he began looking up verses, the Burley twins began to tease him.

"Look at Concord!" Bernie cried. "He thinks that the Bible will say that the sidewalk chalk belongs to Leonard!"

The twins laughed.

"Concord, does the Bible even say anything about chalk?" Leonard asked.

"Actually, I'm not looking up chalk," Concord said as he read a page in the book of Joshua.

"Are you proving that the Burley twins might not really be right-handed?" Leonard asked, confused.

"Nope," Concord replied. "Whether they're left-handed or right-handed doesn't matter." Then Concord's eyes froze on a verse, a grin came to his face, and he tapped his open Bible. "The Burley twins' story can't be true."

"Oh yeah?" the twins said. "Prove it!"

"Read Joshua 10:13-14," he said as he held out the Bible. "It's all the proof we need."

How could Concord prove the twins were lying?

Read Joshua 10:13-14 for the clue that Concord gave the group.

The solution to *"Sidewalk Chalk Talk"* is on page 82.

4
THE PARTY
PIGGY BANK

Concord's class was ten seconds away from being dismissed for the day when Principal Ironsides stepped through the door. The scowling, husky man scanned the class until he spotted Concord.

"Cunningham, I need to see you in my office right after school," he said in his usual gruff tone.

The whole class gasped. The Bible-quoting brain of Pine Tops was the last person anyone expected to be in trouble. The class was so shocked, in fact, that nobody moved when the dismissal bell rang.

Concord was just as surprised as everyone else. A personal invitation from Mr. Ironsides only happened on the most important occasions. Concord took a deep breath and quickly loaded his books into his backpack. As he headed out the door, he received a dozen wishes of "good luck" from fellow students.

By the time he got to Mr. Ironsides' office, he was so nervous that he couldn't stop his nose, of all things, from twitching.

"There you are, Concord," Mr. Ironsides said as he looked up from his desk. "I've got a problem."

"With me?" Concord asked with a gulp and a twitch.

"No, no, no." Mr. Ironsides replied. "You're not in trouble. Sit down, and you'd better relax because it looks like your nose is about to jump off your face."

Concord rubbed his nose and sat down with relief.

"We had some money stolen from Mrs. Pound's classroom this afternoon," Mr. Ironsides said with frustration. "I reported it to the police but they won't be here for about an hour. Chief Riggins said you might be able to figure some things out in the meantime."

Concord nodded. He was glad to help. He was even more glad that he wasn't going to be in detention.

"Let me know what you find out, Mr. Concordance," Principal Ironsides said as he flashed a rare smile, showing his large, bright teeth. Then he caught himself and replaced it with his usual scowl. "Dismissed!"

Concord stood up, spun on his heel, and marched out the door.

When he arrived at Mrs. Pound's classroom, she was sitting at her desk. Not knowing what to say, he paused in the doorway and knocked on the open door.

"Come in, Concord," the short, cheery-faced teacher said. "Mr. Ironsides told me that you were going to try to help us solve this mystery. I just don't know how this could have happened!"

"Hopefully we can figure it out," Concord said. "Let's start from the beginning, Mrs. Pound. Where was the money when it was stolen?"

"In this piggy bank," she said, lifting the bank from her desk. "It always sits right here on the corner of my desk."

"May I see that?" Concord asked. Mrs. Pound handed him the piggy bank.

It was a small piggy bank made out of some kind of clay. The bank was definitely shaped like a pig, but it wasn't professionally done. It looked as if a student had made it. It surprised Concord that the thief hadn't broken open the piggy bank to steal the money. The only opening the bank had was its thin coin slot.

"How much money do you think was in there?"

Concord asked.

"It was almost full," Mrs. Pound sighed. "The class had been saving for a popcorn party. You see, students bring in spare change everyday and drop it into the piggy bank. Yesterday, I told the class the piggy bank was nearly full. That meant we could break it open at the end of the week and use the money for a popcorn party."

"That's a neat idea," Concord commented.

"Oh, it wasn't mine. A student thought it up," she said.

"I see," Concord said, concentrating on the piggy bank. He decided to inspect it more closely. He checked to see if the bank had been broken open and glued back together. Definitely not. There were no cracks. Then he looked for some kind of trap door or secret opening. No luck. Then he looked at the signature on the belly of the pig.

"Rodney Doomsey?"

"Yes. Rodney came up with the idea on pottery day," Mrs. Pound explained. "The students were each given a three-pound lump of clay. They were told to create whatever they wanted. Students made all kinds of things: animals, cars, people, and lots of who-knows-what," she giggled. "Rodney wanted to make a piggy bank so the class could save some money and then have a party. I thought it would be fun, so I agreed to the idea. The class called it the 'party piggy bank.'"

"So when exactly was the money stolen?" asked Concord.

"It had to have happened during the afternoon break," said Mrs. Pound.

"How do you know for sure?" Concord asked.

"Just before the break, a student dropped a quarter in the piggy bank. I heard it hit the other coins in the bank," Mrs. Pound explained. "When the students came back in after the break, another student dropped a quarter in the bank, and we heard it hit the bottom of the bank. All the money was gone!"

"So you were out of the room during the break?" Concord asked.

"I did go down to the restroom to wash my hands, but I was only down there for a minute at the most. I was here the rest of the time," Mrs. Pound said. "I'm sure that's the only chance anybody had to mess with the piggy bank without being seen by me or the rest of the class. And that one minute definitely isn't enough time to shake all that change out of the bank's coin slot."

Concord looked at the thin slot. It was barely wide enough for a quarter to fit through. It might be possible to shake a coin or two out of the coin slot in a minute, but definitely not all the money.

"I agree that shaking it all out wouldn't be possible in such a short time," Concord concluded. "Tell me about the clay. How did the students change it from soft, moldable stuff to this rock-solid surface?" he asked as he tapped the hard piggy bank.

"It's a new product that I just discovered in a catalog," she said proudly. "Usually, after you mold your clay, you put it in a kiln to harden into pottery. But this clay is special. You just stick it in the microwave for ten minutes and it's as hard as a rock. Good thing, too. We don't have a kiln in the school."

Concord looked around the room for a microwave.

"Oh, we don't have a microwave in here, either," she said, knowing what he was looking for. "The students took their clay creations home and microwaved them there. Then they brought them back the next day, and we displayed them over there on the windowsill. All except for Rodney's piggy bank, of course. It's always been right here on my desk to collect money."

Concord slowly paced around the room in thought. He stopped next to the windowsill where all of the clay creations were.

"Mrs. Pound, do you notice any difference between Rodney's piggy bank and these other creations?" he asked.

"Well, they're all different," she said. "I guess Rodney's piggy bank is quite a bit smaller than the other creations. Rodney said that he didn't want to make his piggy bank too big because it would take too long to fill. He was probably hoping for a popcorn party as soon as possible."

Concord's eyes darted back and forth as he thought about the facts. Then he unzipped his backpack and pulled out his Bible.

"I think Rodney knew that there would never be a popcorn party, Mrs. Pound," Concord said.

"What?" Mrs. Pound exclaimed. "You think that Rodney stole the money? How is that possible?"

Concord placed his Bible on Mrs. Pound's desk and opened it to the book of Romans. He flipped over to chapter nine and read for a moment. Then he nodded, apparently having found what he was looking for.

"Please read Romans 9:21," The Concordance said. "You'll see what I mean."

How did Rodney steal the money?

Read Romans 9:21 for the clue that Concord gave Mrs. Pound.

The solution to *"The Party Piggy Bank"* is on page 83.

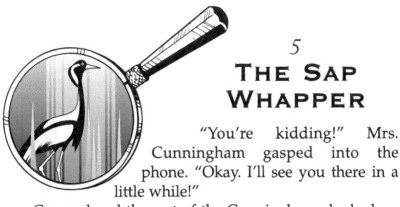

5
THE SAP WHAPPER

"You're kidding!" Mrs. Cunningham gasped into the phone. "Okay. I'll see you there in a little while!"

Concord and the rest of the Cunninghams looked up from their peach pie with curiosity. Mrs. Cunningham turned to them with wide-open eyes.

"That was Betty from the Pine Tops Bird Lover's Society," she said. Mrs. Cunningham was an active member of the society. "Betty says Edmund Lock is winning the 50 year-old Sap Whapper contest tonight."

Concord exchanged puzzled looks with his brother and sister.

"I didn't know there was a 50 year-old contest in Pine Tops," Concord said.

"Oh, yes," his mom began. "The Pine Tops area is the only known habitat of the Hooded Northwest Emperor Pine Sap Whapper."

Mr. Cunningham looked up from his pie. "So people have been trying to catch the Whap Sapper for 50 years?" he asked.

"It's a Sap Whapper," Mrs. Cunningham corrected. "And no, we don't believe in promoting the capture of wild birds."

"So everyone tries to take a picture of the Snap Happer?" asked Concord.

"It's Sap Whapper," she said. The group giggled. "And no, we have many pictures of it."

The pie eaters were confused. Concord's younger sister, Charlotte, finally spoke up. "Then if you're not trying to catch it and you already have a picture of it, what's the Northern Emperor's Whoop Sappy Whap contest about?"

Now the group was in a full-bellied laugh, except for Mrs. Cunningham, who raised her hands to her hips.

"The big deal," she said, "is that no one has ever heard the Hooded Northwest Emperor Pine Sap Whapper sing. For 50 years the Bird Lover's Society has offered a prize for a recording of the Sap Whapper song."

"How big of a prize?" Concord asked.

"The society just increased the amount to one thousand dollars this year," Mrs. Cunningham said. "Since then, all kinds of people have been hiking through the forest with tape recorders."

"Have there been any attempts to claim the prize before now?" asked Mr. Cunningham. He wondered if this might be a possible article for the *Ponderosa Press*.

"There have been a couple," she said, "but the society's expert panel recognized both recordings as other birds. The experts know every bird song there is—except, of course, the Sap Whapper's."

"I think I'd better come with you," Mr. Cunningham said. "This could be a big story for the newspaper if the recording really is the Sap Whapper song."

"What if it's just some other bird again?" asked Concord.

"That's why we're so excited," Mrs. Cunningham replied. She pulled her long brown hair into a ponytail as she got ready to leave. "Mr. Lock, who is claiming the prize, is one of the experts on our panel. He would know if his recording was the wrong bird!"

"Maybe the whole family should come along to hear a piece of Pine Tops history in the making," Mr.

Cunningham proposed.

The family agreed.

When the Cunninghams arrived at the auditorium a few minutes later, it was already packed. Some people were bird lovers. Some wanted to be there when the Sap Whapper song was heard in public for the first time. Some just wanted to finally figure out the crazy name of the bird that everybody was talking about.

After weaving through the crowd, Concord found five seats together and motioned his family over. The Cunninghams sat down just as the lights dimmed. The society's president, Mr. Birk, picked up the microphone on the stage as a spotlight found him. He was dressed in a blue suit for the special occasion.

"Good evening ladies and gentlemen," he said. "Before I hand the microphone over to Edmund Lock and his recording, let me tell you a little bit about the Hooded Northwest Emperor Pine Sap Whapper. It is the rarest bird in the Northwest. It lives by waterfalls. The mist from the waterfalls keeps the Sap Whapper's wings moist so it can whap well. The bird is wonderfully colored with orange, green, yellow, and some purple around the beak."

A slide projector cast an image of the bird on a large screen on the stage.

"Without any further delay," President Birk continued, "may I present Edmund Lock."

The audience clapped with anticipation as Edmund made his way to the microphone.

"Thank you," Edmund said with a smile. He was in his forties, and he wore a flannel shirt, black jeans, and hiking boots. "It's always been a dream of mine to record the song of the Sap Whapper. I've been carrying my tape recorder with me on every forest outing for some time now, just in case.

"Yesterday, my wife and I hiked up to the Grand Pine River Falls. We were right at the base of the waterfall, gazing up at the beautiful, thirty foot-high wall of white water. Suddenly, a Sap Whapper flew through the mist and landed on the tree beside us. It was big. It was a whopper of a Whapper."

The audience chuckled.

"I pulled out my tape recorder. I started recording just as my wife was saying how beautiful the Sap Whapper was. I managed to shush her just in time to hear the most unique bird song I've ever heard."

He held up his tape recorder to the microphone and pressed the play button. The tape echoed through the auditorium speakers.

"Look how beautiful it is, Edmu—"

"Shhhhh."

The tape was silent. And then:

"Kwaaank! Chirp. Toooweeee! Toooweeee! Kwunk, kwunk. Cluck!

   Kwaaank! Chirp. Toooweeee! Toooweeee! Kwunk, kwunk. Cluck!"

The audience jumped to its feet in applause. President Birk walked over to Edmund and patted him on the back.

"Spectacular!" President Birk said. "If I could get the rest of the expert panel on the stage, please. We'll decide if Edmund's recording is the winner of the one thousand dollar prize."

As the other five panel members made their way onto the stage, Concord rubbed his forehead.

"What is it, Concord?" his mother asked.

"Something about this is strange," he said. Concord wasn't sure why, but the recording was reminding him of a psalm that he had been trying to memorize earlier in the week.

On stage, President Birk huddled with the other five panel members. Then, as the panel turned back toward the audience, President Birk picked up the microphone. "Ladies and gentlemen, by a unanimous vote the panel has decided that we have just heard the first-ever recording of the Hooded Northwest Emperor Pine Sap Whapper's song!" President Birk announced.

As the audience applauded in celebration, Concord's eyes froze and his eyebrows rose. He tugged on his mom's shirt.

"It's a fake!" Concord exclaimed.

"The recording?" Mrs. Cunningham asked.

"Yes," Concord said. "You've got to stop them from giving Edmund the prize!"

"But what should I tell President Birk?" Mrs. Cunningham asked. "How do you know?" "Tell Mr. Birk that the evidence is in Psalm 42," The Concordance said. He closed his eyes and searched his memory. "Psalm 42:7 to be exact."

How did Concord know Mr. Lock's recording was a fake?

Read Psalm 42:7 for the clue that Concord gave his mom.

The solution to *"The Sap Whapper"* is on page 84.

6
THE STOLEN FLAMINGO

When Pine Tops radio station KONE-FM interrupted regular programming with a special announcement, it got the town's attention. But that didn't last long. Hearing that the local Sequoia Art Museum had been robbed wasn't very exciting news to most Pine Tops residents. After all, Mrs. Spenkle's paint-dipped pine cones and Mr. Billow's stump collection weren't worth much more than their weight in firewood.

But residents eventually remembered that this was the week that the Sequoia Art Museum had a special display: "White Flamingo." It was created by Wes Turner, a relatively new Pine Tops resident.

The White Flamingo was a sparkling, two-foot tall statue. It was expected to sell for three to seven thousand dollars in an auction that was supposed to be held on the upcoming Saturday. That was a high price for a piece of Pine Tops art. But, the White Flamingo was a dazzling piece of work, at least compared to Mr. Billow's stump collection.

According to the KONE-FM announcement, the White Flamingo had been stolen sometime last night. As usual, the *Ponderosa Press* wanted its best reporter, Mr. Cunningham, to cover the story.

"Thanks for bringing me along, Dad," Concord said as they arrived at the Sequoia Art Museum.

"Sure, Concord," Mr. Cunningham replied. "Chief Riggins said you're always welcome to join me at his crime scenes." They got out of the car and headed for the museum door. "Besides, it never hurts to have The Concordance around."

As they walked through the museum door, their feet squished into the carpet. It was soaking wet! But that wasn't the worst of it. They looked down the walkway ramp into the display area and saw three inches of water covering the floor. In fact, there was water everywhere. The windows were steamed, the walls were glistening, and the art was dripping.

"Welcome to Pine Tops' first indoor swamp!" Chief Riggins shouted across the room.

"What happened, Chief?" Concord asked as he and his dad splashed across the floor.

"Whoever stole the White Flamingo decided to set off the fire sprinklers in the ceiling," the chief said. "The sprinklers were going all night because nobody knew they were running; the wire to the fire bell was cut."

"So the sprinklers went off but the alarm didn't," Mr. Cunningham said to himself as he began to write the facts down in his reporter's notebook.

"Do you think they were trying to wash away fingerprints and evidence?" asked Concord.

"Could be," the chief said as he tried to wring out the cuffs of his pants. "What does the Bible have to say about floods, anyway?"

"Genesis 7:24," Concord smirked. "The waters flooded the earth for a hundred and fifty days."

"I hope we don't see history repeat itself," Mr. Cunningham chuckled. "I'd hate to see Mr. Billows stump collection get waterlogged."

The group enjoyed a laugh.

Mr. Cunningham looked back at his notepad. "What else have you got, Chief?" he asked.

"Well, the museum has a rather nice vault to store valuable items—on the rare occasion that they're here," the chief chuckled. "The White Flamingo was in the vault last night when it was stolen. The museum director, Mr. Blazer, says that yesterday was like any other day. After the museum closed, he moved the statue from the display floor to the vault, which he locked. Then he went home, and he was there the rest of the night with his wife. He's positive that he's the only one with the combination to the vault."

"So the vault was broken into?" Concord asked.

"We're not sure," said the chief. "We haven't found any signs that the vault was forced open."

"Do you think somebody figured out the combination?" Concord asked.

"I don't think so," said the chief. "Mr. Blazer says that the combination has five numbers in it. I don't see how anybody could figure that out. Even if there is some superstar robber who can do that sort of thing, I doubt that he or she would be here in the Sequoia Art Museum. The payoff isn't big enough."

"So how else could a robber have stolen the statue out of the vault?" Mr. Cunningham asked.

"We don't know yet," Chief Riggins said. "All we know is that when Mr. Blazer opened the vault this morning, the White Flamingo was gone. All that was in there was sprinkler water."

"The vault has a sprinkler, too?" Mr. Cunningham asked.

"Yep," the chief confirmed. "I guess it's in case a fire breaks out in there."

"So do you have any suspects, Chief?" Concord asked.

"Actually, we do," the chief said as his brow tightened. "We suspect the artist himself. We just got a call from Pine Tops Insurance Agency. Wes Turner, the artist, took out a seven thousand dollar insurance policy on the White Flamingo just two days ago.

"We know that statue was supposed to sell for between three and seven thousand dollars at this Saturday's auction. Of course, with an auction, you never know for sure what price you're going to get. The statue could sell for only two or three thousand. We think Mr. Turner might have stolen the statue so he could get the seven thousand dollars for sure."

"Is that the only evidence you have against him?" Mr. Cunningham asked.

"No," said the chief. "A witness thinks she saw him behind the museum last night. That's where the wire to the fire alarm was cut. It's also where somebody threw a smoke bomb through a museum window to set off the fire sprinklers."

"But even if he was the vandal who cut the alarm bell wire and then set off the sprinklers, how could he have stolen the statue?" Mr. Cunningham challenged.

"We don't know," the chief sighed. "And if we can't prove that he stole the White Flamingo, he'll get the insurance money."

"Since the museum director is the only one with access to the vault, how can you be sure it wasn't him?" asked Mr. Cunningham.

"The Sequoia Art Museum is just one of many establishments that Mr. Blazer owns. He's very wealthy. A statue like this is small potatoes for him. Besides, it wouldn't make sense for him to steal it. Nobody will ever want to bring any valuable art here again. His reputation and business will be hurt. But you can talk to him if you wish. He's right over there." The chief pointed to a stocky, older man with dark-rimmed glasses who was standing in the middle of the display floor.

The Cunninghams sloshed over to Mr. Blazer.

"Craziest thing I've ever seen," Mr. Blazer said. "Maybe I should turn this place into a boat museum."

"Mr. Blazer, I'm Mr. Cunningham from the *Ponderosa Press*, and this is my son, Concord. For the record, are you sure that you locked the vault last night?" Mr. Cunningham asked.

"Absolutely positive," Mr. Blazer confirmed. "I stood the White Flamingo in the middle of the vault's floor and then immediately closed and locked the door. When I opened the vault this morning, it was like being hit by a tidal wave. There isn't any kind of drain in that vault, so it filled up with water like a bath tub."

The group started walking towards the vault. Chief Riggins followed.

"Was the wave big enough to sweep the White Flamingo out of the vault when the door was opened?" Concord asked.

"I thought of that, too," Mr. Blazer answered. "I looked around but the statue wasn't anywhere."

When they arrived at the vault, Concord and his dad stepped inside it. Concord looked at the vault's walls. They were solid concrete. So was the floor. And so was the ceiling. Concord inspected the lock, and it seemed to be in perfect condition.

Concord looked over to Mr. Blazer, "Did you ever tell anyone the combination?"

"Not a soul. And I always made sure that no one was watching when I opened the vault," Mr. Blazer boasted.

Mr. Cunningham continued to take notes. "Did the artist ever say anything about his insurance on the statue?" he asked.

"Not that I recall," said Mr. Blazer. "But I'm not surprised that he had insurance. The statue was very lightweight and seemed very fragile. When he saw me move it into the vault for the first time, he kept telling me how careful I had to be with it. He followed me all the way into the vault to make sure I didn't drop it."

Chief Riggins was about to ask Mr. Blazer a question, but Mr. Blazer seemed to read his mind.

"I know what you're thinking, Chief," Mr. Blazer said. "But the vault was already open that day. The artist didn't have a chance to watch me dial the combination."

The chief exhaled and nodded. Meanwhile, Concord looked around the vault for other clues. Nothing. In fact, all of the vault's shelves were empty, as usual.

Then Concord noticed a small puddle of water on one of the vault's warped lower shelves. The puddle was leftover from when the vault had been filled with water. Concord dipped his finger into the water and tasted it. His eyes lit up.

As Mr. Cunningham talked to Mr. Blazer and Chief Riggins, Concord pulled his Bible out of his backpack. Somehow, the water had given him an idea.

Mr. Blazer looked over at Concord, who had begun rustling through Bible pages.

"What's he doing?" Mr. Blazer asked.

"It's looks like he's working on the case," Chief Riggins said with a grin.

The chief winked at Mr. Cunningham. Mr. Cunningham grinned back.

"He's working on the case with a Bible?" Mr. Blazer asked, confused.

Chief Riggins and Mr. Cunningham nodded.

A moment later, Concord turned to the group. "The chief was right. The artist stole the White Flamingo to get the insurance money," he said.

"But how?" Mr. Blazer exclaimed.

"He was quite creative," said The Concordance. "Genesis 19:26 helps explain how he did it."

How did the artist do it?

Read Genesis 19:26 for the clue that Concord gave Mr. Blazer.

The solution to *"The Stolen Flamingo"* is on page 85.

7
REDHEAD ROCKS

What are you doing for lunch today?" Charlie Lowman asked Concord as they walked toward the school cafeteria.

"I'm going to try my luck with the pizza," Concord said. "How about you?"

"I'm using my lunch money to buy a rock," Charlie replied.

"A rock?" Concord repeated with a raised eyebrow. "Won't that be a little hard on your stomach?"

"It would be if I ate it," Charlie said. "But I'd have to be crazy to eat a Redhead rock."

Concord laughed. "You'd have to be crazy to eat any rock," he said. Then he realized what Charlie had just said. Concord stopped walking and turned to his messy-haired friend. "You're buying a real Redhead rock?" Concord asked.

"That's right," said Charlie. "You might be able to buy one, too. A couple of guys in my class said they'd be selling Redhead rocks on the playground at lunch today."

Redhead rocks were found in only one place: the very top of Mount Redhead. The towering mountain could be seen from just about anywhere in Pine Tops. Its bottom half was covered with thick pine trees. Above the tree line, the mountain had steep granite slopes and cliffs. And at the tip of Mount Redhead's sharp peak was a patch of dark red rock, the location of Redhead rocks.

Since Mount Redhead was so tall and difficult to climb, Redhead rocks were extremely hard to get. In fact, they were considered a treasure in Pine Tops. A climber who made it to the top of Mount Redhead never failed to bring back a Redhead rock as a trophy of his or her accomplishment.

Redhead rock owners frequently got offers from folks who wanted to buy their rocks. However, sales rarely took place. Most people wouldn't even think of selling the Redhead rocks they had worked so hard to get, at least until today.

"How much are they selling the rocks for?" Concord asked Charlie.

"They said one dollar per rock," Charlie said.

"I think I'd better go with you," said Concord. "That sounds too good to be true. But just in case it isn't, let's go before I spend my money on that pizza."

It wasn't hard to find the rock sale. There was a large crowd of students around two boys standing on a bench. As Charlie and Concord walked closer, Concord recognized the boys on the bench.

"The Burley twins," Concord sighed. "Now I'm really suspicious."

"Ladies and gentlemen!" Bart Burley cried out to the crowd. "In this backpack are the most wanted rocks in Pine Tops. For only one dollar, you can be the envy of everyone you know. You can be the owner of a genuine Redhead rock!"

Charlie whispered to Concord, "I hope they're real. I'm going to get one for my dad. He always looks at Mount Redhead out our back window and says someday he's going to get a Redhead rock. He won't believe it when I hand him one!"

A student in the crowd called out, "How do we know

they're real?"

Bernie Burley answered, "My brother Bart and I spent our whole Saturday climbing Mount Redhead with this backpack, so we could bring back these rocks. Tell me if these look real to you." He held up one of the dark red rocks for all to see. A few students clapped while others nodded in approval.

Concord made his way through the crowd to get a closer look. Bart Burley saw him approach.

"Ladies and gentlemen!" Bart shouted. "Look who wants to be the very first customer! It's none other than The Concordance."

Eyes shifted from Bart to Concord.

"May I see the rock?" Concord asked.

"For the low, low price of one dollar you can have it," Bart replied.

"I'll definitely buy it if it's real," Concord assured him. "But I'd like to look at it first to make sure it is."

Bart looked over at Bernie. Bernie nodded and then yelled to the crowd, "We will now have The Concordance inspect the rock to show everyone that these are real Redhead rocks!" The twins nodded at each other. They knew that if Concord said the Redhead rocks were real, the rock sale would be a smashing success.

Bart handed the rock over to Concord. It was a beautiful, dark red rock.

Concord looked across the school yard and up at Mount Redhead. The sun was shining on the mountain's majestic, dark red peak. Concord looked back at the rock. The color of the rock perfectly matched the color of Mount Redhead's tip.

Charlie leaned over to Concord. "Was it painted?" he asked.

Concord tilted his head. "I can't tell for sure," he said.

43

"They might have spray painted it, but it's hard to say."

"So they might be telling the truth!" Charlie said excitedly. The crowd started to buzz with hope.

"Of course we're telling the truth!" Bernie Burley shouted. "Wouldn't the great Concordance know if we weren't?"

Concord rubbed his thumb around the smooth, round rock to see if any paint would come off. None did. He still suspected that it had been painted, but he couldn't prove it.

"So how about that dollar, Mr. Concordance?" Bernie said as he held out his hand.

After a short pause, Concord began to pull his lunch money out of his pocket. Suddenly, he stopped and looked at the rock. His eyes flashed to the side and then back to the rock. He had just remembered something from one of his favorite Bible stories: David and Goliath.

Instead of giving Bernie a dollar, Concord handed him the rock. Then Concord dropped his backpack to the ground and pulled out his Bible.

"That was close," Concord said as he flipped the pages. "I almost bought that rock instead of pizza."

"But isn't the rock worth more than a piece of pizza?" Charlie asked.

"Nope," Concord said as he found the page he was seeking. "There's no way that rock came from the top of Mount Redhead."

"Of course it did!" Bernie cried out to the crowd, trying to save the rock sale. "You can all see for yourself, just look up at Mount Redhead. What makes you think the rocks came from anywhere else?"

Concord held his Bible up in the air. "Anyone who wants to buy one of those rocks should read 1 Samuel 17:40," The

Concordance announced to the crowd. "It proves that the rocks must have come from somewhere else."

How did Concord know the rocks were not real Redhead rocks?

Read 1 Samuel 17:40 for the clue Concord gave the crowd.

The solution to *"Redhead Rocks"* is on page 86.

8
THE COLLAPSING CRACKERS

Walking home from school is never dull for Concord. Kids of all ages stroll alongside him, hoping to get answers to their questions. Concord doesn't mind. In fact, he rather enjoys the challenge.

"Did a guy really live inside a fish for three days?" a kid asked one day.

"Yep," Concord confirmed. "Read Jonah, chapters one and two."

Another asked, "Was Noah's ark real?"

"You bet," Concord said. "It's in Genesis, chapter six."

"Are dogs really color blind?" another asked.

Concord chuckled. "You'll have to check your science book for that one," he said. He knew better than to try answering something that he didn't know for sure.

Concord's walk home this day included a stop at the Pine Tops Youth Center. His sister, Charlotte, had advanced to the finals of the youth center's most popular contest: the graham cracker cabin-building competition.

Last night, Charlotte and a dozen other contestants were each given ten boxes of graham crackers, a bowl of frosting, and one hour to build the most spectacular cracker cabin they could. Mr. Bobbin, the youth center director, chose two finalists at the end of the hour. This year, they were Charlotte Cunningham and Rodney Doomsey.

Today, two announcers from KONE-FM were coming to the youth center to decide which of the two finalists would be the winner. The winner's name would then be broadcast on a special KONE-FM report. Meanwhile, the youth center crowd would enjoy the annual tradition of eating all the losing entries.

Concord arrived just as a dozen other hungry spectators shuffled into the youth center. Concord made his way across the room to his red-headed sister, and he wished her good luck.

"I guess you haven't heard," Charlotte replied angrily as she crossed her freckled arms.

"Heard what?" Concord asked.

"Look!" she shouted, pointing at the window into Mr. Bobbin's office. Yesterday, she and Rodney had each put their cracker cabins in Mr. Bobbin's office to be safely locked up for the night.

Concord looked through the window. He saw two tables in the back of the office that had been reserved for the two cracker cabin finalists. On one table rested a towering cracker creation complete with windows, doors, and a deck off the back. On the other table was a heap of collapsed crackers.

"Is that one yours?" Concord gasped.

"It was mine," Charlotte snarled, "until Rodney Doomsey ruined it so his cracker cabin would win."

Concord checked the doorknob. It was locked. He looked at the office window. It didn't open. There weren't any other doors or windows into the office.

"Are you sure Rodney did that?" Concord asked his sister. "There's no way in."

"It must have been him!" Charlotte insisted. "When I put my cracker cabin in the office last night, the icing had already dried and the cracker cabin was rock-solid. There's no way my cabin could have fallen on its own."

Just then, Rodney Doomsey approached the pair. He wore an oversized hockey jersey and a crooked grin.

"Looks like the judges' decision is going to be real tough," Rodney said with a laugh.

"Rodney, where were you last night?" Concord asked.

"You think I did this?" Rodney asked, his tone changing to serious. "I couldn't have. Mr. Bobbin locked his office for the night right after Charlotte and I put our cracker cabins in there. You could see through the office window that both cabins were still standing when Mr. Bobbin locked the door."

Concord looked over at Charlotte. "Is that true, Charlotte?" Concord asked.

"Yes," Charlotte said with a shrug.

"Right after that," Rodney continued, "we all left and the youth center was closed for the night. It didn't open again until just a few minutes ago when Mr. Bobbin arrived and let us all in. But he hasn't even unlocked his office yet today. He just unlocked the youth center doors when he arrived and then ran down the street to KONE-FM to get the judges."

Concord looked over at Charlotte.

"That's true, too," Charlotte said, grudgingly.

"See? It couldn't have been me," Rodney said with a smile returning to his face. "It couldn't have been anyone. No one has been in the office since it was locked last night, right after we put our cracker cabins in there. Charlotte's cabin must have collapsed all by itself."

"You never answered my question, though, Rodney," Concord politely reminded him.

"If you have to know where I was last night, I was off playing football at Evergreen Park," Rodney said. "Lots of people saw me there. How could they miss me? I scored three amazing touchdowns."

A few kids had gathered to listen to the conversation. They told Concord that they had seen Rodney in the park last night. They also confirmed that Rodney was playing football, but they didn't think his touchdowns were that amazing.

Then a commotion stirred at the youth center door. Mr. Bobbin had arrived with the judges. A number of kids flocked to the bald youth director, telling him about the collapse of Charlotte's cabin. He made his way back to his office and peered through the window.

"Oh, my!" he cried.

"Mr. Bobbin, have you been in your office since you locked the door last night when the cracker cabins were put in there?" Concord asked.

"No, I haven't," Mr. Bobbin said.

Concord believed him. Mr. Bobbin would never damage a kid's project.

"Do you have the only key to the office?" Concord asked.

"Yes, I do," said Mr. Bobbin.

"Was the key ever out of your possession during the past twenty-four hours?" asked Concord.

"Nope. It's on my key ring," he said. "I'd know if it was gone because I need my keys for my car, my house, everything." He held up his key ring and jingled it to show he still had it. "This is such a shame. Both kids worked so hard on their cabins. They showed such determination. Rodney even tripped on a chair yesterday afternoon and thought he had sprained his ankle. But that didn't stop him from finishing his cabin."

"I thought you played football last night, Rodney." Concord challenged.

"Oh, well, uh, yeah. So?" Rodney said as he fidgeted. "My ankle felt better by then."

"It never really swelled up," Mr. Bobbin said. "I gave Rodney some ice to wrap around the ankle right away."

Concord turned back to Mr. Bobbin. "Mr. Bobbin, whose cracker cabin was taken into your office first?" he asked.

"Charlotte took hers in first," he replied. "I remember because Rodney surprised me with his manners. 'Ladies first!' he said."

Concord looked through the office window. As he compared Rodney's cabin to Charlotte's collapsed cabin, he decided to look something up in his Bible. He pulled it out of his backpack and turned to the book of Luke.

Concord murmured to himself, "Only one cracker cabin collapsed, and the two cabins were on separate tables." He rustled through the pages. Soon he found the verse he was seeking, and he turned to Rodney.

"Rodney, I think you faked your injury," Concord said.

"Why would I do that?" Rodney protested.

"Concord," Charlotte interrupted, "even if Rodney faked his injury, it doesn't help me prove that he destroyed my graham cracker cabin."

"To the contrary," Concord proclaimed, "it shows that he planned it all along."

"I'm not sure that I follow," said Mr. Bobbin.

"It was a clever scheme, but Luke 6:49 helps describe what happened," The Concordance said as he handed Mr. Bobbin the opened Bible.

After reading Luke 6:49, Mr. Bobbin unlocked his office door. He walked over to the table that Charlotte's collapsed cracker cabin was on. He looked closely at the cracker heap, felt it, and then announced, "Rodney Doomsey, you are disqualified for cheating!"

How did Rodney ruin Charlotte's graham cracker house?

Read Luke 6:49 for the clue that Concord gave the Mr. Bobbin.

The solution to *"Collapsing Crackers"* is on page 87.

9
THE DAWN
SKIMMER
CHALLENGE

"Hey Concord, up and at 'em," Mr. Cunningham said as he knocked on Concord's bedroom door. Concord rolled over in his bed, looked at the clock, and tried to go back to sleep. He thought he was having a bad dream.

But he wasn't. Mr. Cunningham cracked open the door and tried again. "Anybody alive in there?" he asked, this time a little louder.

Concord could only muster enough energy to mutter two words, "It's Saturday."

"I know," Mr. Cunningham said. He walked in and sat on the bed. "But you said you wanted to go with me the next time I reported a story on a Saturday."

Concord's eyes opened halfway, and he checked his clock again. "I didn't realize it would happen at five in the morning," he groaned.

"Neither did I, but my editor just called me," Mr. Cunningham said with a yawn. Then he looked out the bedroom window. "We've only got about an hour before sunrise, so we have to hurry."

"What's happening at sunrise?" Concord asked as he sat up, rubbing his eyes.

"The Dawn Skimmers will be paddling across Bigwood Lake," Mr. Cunningham said.

The Dawn Skimmers were a group of Pine Tops men who raced canoes.

"But they're out there every Saturday morning at dawn,"

Concord said. "What is there to report?"

"Mayor Ritzo called the newspaper a half-hour ago," Mr. Cunningham explained. "The mayor says he's going to race the Dawn Skimmers across the lake, and he's using a rowboat."

Concord perked up. "The mayor is racing the Dawn Skimmers?" he asked. Then he chuckled, knowing the mayor was the clumsiest man in town. "He must have a motor on the rowboat."

"No motor," Mr. Cunningham said. "And the mayor really thinks he's going to win. At least, he convinced my editor of that."

Concord slowly peeled off the covers. "I guess the mayor must have something up his sleeve. If he didn't, he probably wouldn't risk embarrassing himself," he said.

"That's exactly what my editor thought," Mr. Cunningham said with a nod. "So would you like to come?"

Concord got out of bed and headed for his closet. "Definitely," he said with a yawn.

After they got dressed and ate a quick breakfast, father and son were on their way to Bigwood Lake. When they arrived, the Dawn Skimmers and Mayor Ritzo were already on the beach.

"Looks like the newspaper is covering the mayor's challenge," one of the Dawn Skimmers said as the Cunninghams approached the group.

"Yep," another Skimmer said. "Fine by me. The whole town will get to read how fast the Dawn Skimmers really are."

The mayor sat with a confident grin on his face.

The Cunninghams greeted all the boaters with handshakes. Then Mr. Cunningham began asking questions for his newspaper article.

"Mayor Ritzo, do you really think you can row

across Bigwood Lake faster than the Dawn Skimmers can paddle?" he asked. "They have two people per canoe, you know."

"I know," the mayor said as he stroked his black beard. "But I think I can beat them. I'm tired of this town talking about how clumsy I am. If I can beat the Dawn Skimmers, maybe people will start talking about something else."

"Besides a big headline in the *Ponderosa Press*, what does the winner of the race get?" Mr. Cunningham asked.

Captain Rutwell of the Dawn Skimmers stepped forward. He stood as straight as a soldier, and he had the haircut to match. "If we win," he said, "the mayor is going to take us all out to dinner."

"And if I win," the mayor said, "the Dawn Skimmers are going to help me hang campaign posters all over town for this year's election."

"What are the rules?" Concord asked.

"All of us Dawn Skimmers will be in our canoes," Captain Rutwell said. "The mayor will be in a normal rowboat. Whoever is the first to tie his boat to McCall's Dock on the other side of the lake is the winner. Oh yeah, I almost forgot. No motors allowed, Mr. Mayor."

A few of the Dawn Skimmers laughed and shook their heads, knowing the mayor didn't have a chance without a motor.

"To make this interesting," the mayor said, "and to give Mr. Cunningham a great story for the paper, I'm going to beat the Dawn Skimmers by using only one oar."

The Dawn Skimmers roared in laughter. Some of them began yelling out what they were going to have the mayor buy them for dinner.

Captain Rutwell stepped closer to the mayor. "Ah, did you hear what I said about no motors being allowed?" he asked.

"Most definitely," the mayor assured him. "But, since I'm taking only one oar, would it be all right with you if I brought along the hammer and tarp that are in the rowboat?"

Captain Rutwell walked over to the rowboat and looked at the hammer and tarp. Then he circled the rowboat. He even looked under the boat to make sure there wasn't a secret motor.

"The hammer and the tarp are okay with me," Captain Rutwell said. He was satisfied that everything else was normal. "It's just more weight to slow you down."

Mr. Cunningham had been taking notes on everything that had been happening. "This is going to be a great story," he said to Concord. "I feel sorry for the mayor, though. There's no way he's going to beat the Dawn Skimmers, especially with only one oar. I don't know what he's thinking."

Concord looked up at the trees swaying in the wind. "Dad, did the mayor tell you about this race before today, or did he just decide to do it this morning?" he asked.

"It was a spur of the moment thing from what I understand," Mr. Cunningham said. "He called the paper at about four o'clock this morning to let us know about his challenge."

Concord looked back up at the trees. "He probably decided to challenge the Dawn Skimmers after he heard this morning's weather report," he said.

"What?" Mr. Cunningham said.

Suddenly a starter's gun went off and the race was underway. The Dawn Skimmer teams pushed their canoes into the choppy water and started stroking. Mayor Ritzo grabbed his one oar and pushed the rowboat into the water. But he didn't start paddling. Instead, he grabbed the hammer and started hitting the wooden bench in the middle of his boat.

"What is he doing?" Mr. Cunningham asked in confusion.

"He thinks this morning's wind is moving faster than the Dawn Skimmers can paddle," Concord said.

"What?" Mr. Cunningham questioned.

With one last hit, the major had punched a hole through the rowboat's wooden bench. Then he stood the oar on end and pushed it through the hole. It was standing straight up in the air.

"He's making a sailboat!" Mr. Cunningham shouted. "Go Mayor Ritzo! This is unbelievable. He might actually win. This will be a front page story for sure!"

The mayor tied the tarp along the length of the oar. Then, with one big tug, he tied the other end of the tarp to the side of the boat. The sail was complete. It filled with air, and the rowboat shot out into the lake.

The time it took Mayor Ritzo to make the sailboat had given the Dawn Skimmers a four minute head start. But the mayor was quickly gaining on them.

"He might just beat them!" Mr. Cunningham cried as he looked across the lake. "It looks like the mayor's clumsy image could be about to change. Let's get back to the car so we can drive around the lake to McCall's Dock and see who wins the race."

The Cunninghams hurried back to their car and were soon driving toward the other side of Bigwood Lake. As they zoomed through the trees that grew beside the shore, Concord thought about the mayor's homemade sailboat.

Concord pulled his backpack up from the car's floor to his lap and took out his Bible. He then turned to the concordance section, and he began looking up verses about ships.

A few minutes later, Mr. Cunningham heard Concord say, "Uh-oh."

"What is it?" Mr. Cunningham asked.

"I don't think the mayor is going to win this race, Dad," Concord replied as he looked up from his Bible.

"Why not?" his dad asked. "As long as the wind keeps up he might have a chance. The lake is a couple miles across, so he has plenty of time to catch the Dawn Skimmers."

"Mayor Ritzo should have read James 3:4," The Concordance said. "The Dawn Skimmers are going to get to McCall's Dock first."

How did Concord know that the mayor would lose the race to McCall's Dock?

Read James 3:4 for the clue that Concord gave his dad.

The solution to *"The Dawn Skimmer Challenge"* is on page 88.

10
TOPLESS TREES

Concord had always thought it was funny. The two most famous pine trees in Pine Tops didn't have tops at all. The painted trees, as they were known, had been topless since they were struck in the famous lightning storm of 1913.

For some reason, nobody had ever bothered to chop them down. Eventually, when the trees died, the town of Pine Tops decided to paint giant people on the dead, grey, forty-foot tall tree trunks. Since the topless trees were near the highway, the painted characters greeted folks driving into Pine Tops.

"Who do you think they painted on the trees this time?" Charlie Lowman asked Concord. The two friends were riding their bikes to the unveiling ceremony.

"Hopefully not lumberjacks," Concord said. "They paint those almost every year."

"I'm hoping for a space alien," Charlie said, "with glow-in-the-dark paint!"

"That could be interesting," Concord chuckled. "Can you imagine driving along a highway at night and suddenly seeing a forty-foot tall space alien?"

Charlie shrugged. "My Uncle Red said that happened to him just last week."

The boys laughed.

As they neared the painted trees, they saw that quite a crowd had gathered. But rather than celebrating the newly painted trees, most people were shaking their heads in disgust.

Concord wasn't sure why at first. The first tree was painted like a lumberjack, as usual. Then he saw the second tree and he understood. It was an exact replica of Pine Tops Mayor Ritzo, except for one thing: the mayor that was painted on the tree trunk had chickenpox all over him.

"Didn't Mayor Ritzo have chickenpox last year?" Charlie asked Concord.

"Sure did," Concord said, staring at the tree.

"Hard to believe somebody would embarrass the mayor like that," Charlie said.

"Yeah," Concord agreed, "especially when there's prize money on the line for the best painted tree."

"How much does the winner get?" Charlie asked.

"Five hundred dollars," Concord replied. He rubbed his chin, looking over at the judges. "No judge is going to vote for a tree that makes fun of the mayor."

"Sounds kind of suspicious," Charlie said.

The Concordance nodded in agreement.

Concord and Charlie made their way through the crowd to get a closer look at the painted trees. The lumberjack tree was nicely done, but the mayor tree was more detailed and colored better. It certainly would have won, had there been no chickenpox.

"Pretty ridiculous looking, isn't it?" said a short man standing next to them. "I can't believe she did that to my painting and got away with it."

"You're the painter of the mayor tree?" Concord asked.

"Yeah," he said. "I'm Dwayne Brown. Nice to meet you." He tipped his wide-brimmed hat at the boys.

"Concord Cunningham," Concord said, holding out his hand. "This is Charlie Lowman."

They all shook hands.

"Concord?" Mr. Brown questioned. "Are you the kid they call 'The Concordance?'"

"That's him," Charlie replied. "He's never met a mystery the Bible couldn't solve."

"Then maybe you can help me out," Mr. Brown said. "Everybody thinks I'm just a sore loser for saying this, but I didn't put those chickenpox on the mayor."

"So you're saying that there was foul play," Concord said.

Charlie giggled at the pun. Concord tried his best to keep from smiling, but couldn't stop a big grin from creeping across his face.

"Sorry," Concord apologized. "I know this isn't funny."

"That's okay," Mr. Brown said. "But yes, there was foul play. This was done to my tree so I would lose the contest. I know that Cheryl Riley, the other tree painter, must have done it."

"Cheryl Riley, the pitcher on the Pine Tops softball team?" Charlie asked.

"Yep," Mr. Brown said.

"Why are you so sure it was Cheryl?" Concord asked.

"Because of the way the contest worked," Mr. Brown said. "The painted trees were covered with parachutes until today. Each parachute was staked down like a tent over each tree trunk. That way, nobody could see what we were painting. Anyway, I saw my painting of Mayor Ritzo five minutes before the painted trees were unveiled to the crowd. Those chickenpox weren't there."

"What makes you think Mrs. Riley was the one that put them there." Concord asked.

"Both tents were being watched by a few of the local, retired policemen," Mr. Brown explained. "They say that nobody was allowed in the tents during those last five minutes."

"Nobody at all?" Concord asked.

"There was one exception," Mr. Brown explained. "It's part of the contest tradition. The two tree painters get to sneak a peak at the each other's tree right before the parachute tents are taken off. So, five minutes before these trees were unveiled, I went into Mrs. Riley's tent to look at her tree, and she went into my tent."

"And when you came out, the parachutes were pulled off, and your tree had chickenpox," Concord concluded.

"Right," Mr. Brown confirmed.

"So why didn't anyone believe you when you said that she did it?" Charlie asked.

"The audience thought I was just making excuses when it turned out that nobody liked the chicken pox. Plus, look how high up those chickenpox go," Mr. Brown said.

"All the way to the top," Charlie observed.

"Right," Mr. Brown said. "The ladders had already been taken out of the tents when we visited each other's tree."

"So everybody thinks that only you could have done it, back when the ladders were in there," Concord said. "If that's not true, how do you think she did it?" Concord asked.

"I found this on the ground," Mr. Brown said. He held up a stick with a sponge stuck on the end of it.

Concord touched the sponge. It still had wet red paint on it.

"She must have used the stick so she wouldn't get paint on her hands," Mr. Brown said. "But it isn't long enough to reach up to the top," Concord said. "That's about forty feet up there. The stick is only two or three feet long."

"Could she have stood on anything else in your tent?" Charlie asked.

"Not really," Mr. Brown answered. "There were still a few cans of paint in there, including red. But they would have only stacked up to about three feet. Even if she stood on those, she couldn't have reached very high."

Concord rubbed his chin as he considered the evidence.

"What if she just threw the sponge up there?" Charlie asked. "She is a softball player."

"You must not have seen her lately," Mr. Brown said. He looked through the crowd and spotted her. "She's right over there by the other tree, getting her picture taken."

Concord and Charlie looked over at Mrs. Riley and saw what Mr. Brown meant. She had casts on her right arm and right leg.

"She was in a car accident a couple months ago," Mr. Brown said. "Her sister helped her finish her tree. But Cheryl was still the only one who went in my tent for the sneak peak."

"Looks like the softball team is in trouble this year," Charlie said. "That's her throwing arm."

"Exactly," Mr. Brown said. "Everybody knows that she can't throw with her left, so she couldn't have thrown the sponge forty feet up the tree trunk."

"She couldn't have climbed the tree, either," Concord thought out loud.

Mrs. Riley noticed that they were looking at her. She slowly hobbled over, using a walking stick.

"Oh great. Here she comes," Mr. Brown said as she approached.

"I'm so sorry the crowd didn't like your attempt at political humor, Dwayne," she said with a smirk.

"Don't you mean your attempt, Cheryl," Mr. Brown replied.

"Are you still trying to say that I put those chicken pox on your tree?" she said with a laugh. "Why, anyone can see that I'm in no condition to do that."

"Excuse me, Mrs. Riley," Concord said, "I couldn't help noticing that you're using a walking stick instead of crutches."

"Yes," she said. "My armpits were a little sore from those crutches, so I thought I'd use a walking stick today."

"It looks a little green," Concord said. "Doesn't it bend when you lean on it?"

"Sure, but I don't mind," she said. "The green ones don't break as easily."

Concord's eyes started darting back and forth.

"Hey Concord," Charlie called from a few feet away. "Look what I found. Is this a clue?"

Concord walked over to inspect. It was a shoelace.

Concord grinned at Charlie. "I think this may be the missing piece to the puzzle, Charlie," he said.

Concord glanced at Mrs. Riley's left foot. "Mrs. Riley, are you missing a shoelace?"

Mrs. Riley had a worried look on her face. She looked down at the empty shoelace holes in her shoe. "I suppose I am," she said cautiously.

"Mr. Brown, you'd better go get the judges," Concord said. "We can prove Mrs. Riley had a way to put those chickenpox on your tree."

"No way!" Mrs. Riley said angrily. "How dare you accuse me of doing that? There's no way I could have climbed that tree or thrown paint up there. "

"According to Psalm 11:2," The Concordance said, "there is a way."

How did Cheryl Riley put chickenpox on the tree trunk?

Read Psalm 11:2 for Concord's clue.

The solution to *"Topless Trees"* is on page 89.

11
RIVER
RASPBERRIES

"Hey Concord!" Logan Lifton yelled across the crowded school hall. "You're not going to believe the deal I made with the Burley twins!"

"Uh-oh," Concord thought to himself. When it came to deals with the Burley twins, there was no such thing as a good one.

Logan's black, spiked hair bobbed through a sea of students as he made his way over to Concord's locker.

"How hungry are you?" Logan asked as he arrived.

"I could eat my math book if I had some salt," Concord joked.

"Naw, books are only good with ketchup," Logan joked back. "You know what's even better?"

"What?" Concord asked, expecting an even crazier suggestion.

"Wild raspberries," Logan said with a serious grin.

"Can't argue with you there," Concord agreed. Then he raised his eyebrows. "You have some?"

"Not just some, a whole patch of them," Logan boasted.

"No way!" Concord gasped. "Where'd you find them?"

"Actually, the Burley twins found them," Logan explained. "But they gave all picking and eating rights to me."

"That's pretty generous of them," Concord said suspiciously. "Were you out wild raspberry hunting with the Burley twins?"

"Nope," Logan said. "My class went on a field trip

today. We were on the banks of the Grand Pine River trying to identify plants. I was working on my assignment when the Burley twins called me over. They were sitting on two logs on the bank of the river. There was a whole patch of wild raspberries right next to the logs."

"And the Burley twins decided to give you all the raspberries?" Concord asked.

"Well, not exactly," Logan said. "They said that if I helped them identify all the plants on the field trip assignment I could have all rights to the raspberry plants next to the logs."

"Hmm," Concord pondered. "And you accepted the deal?"

"Sure did! Want to go check it out?" Logan asked excitedly.

"Why not," Concord said. "I love wild raspberries!"

Concord put his homework in his backpack, grabbed his bike helmet, and they were off.

It was about a fifteen minute bike ride to where Logan's biology class had been.

"I'm even hungrier now," Logan said as they approached the river. "I think we're pretty close." He stopped his bike and scanned up and down the riverbank, looking for the two logs that marked the raspberry patch. "There they are!"

Logan got off his bike and ran over to the logs. He froze. "Where'd the raspberries go?" he cried. "They were right here!"

Concord and Logan scurried around the logs. There were plenty of plants and bushes, but not a raspberry in sight.

"Are you sure there were raspberries here?" Concord asked.

"Definitely," Logan insisted. "I ate one myself. It was right next to these logs."

Suddenly, they heard two voices in the distance. Concord looked up and saw Bart and Bernie Burley about two hundred feet upstream on the river bank.

"How are those wild raspberries?" Bart yelled with a laugh. "Sure hope they were worth all of the answers to the biology assignment."

"By the way," Bernie yelled, "thanks, Logan. We got A's on our assignments!"

The twins slapped their knees as they laughed.

Logan looked over at Concord. "What are they doing here?" he asked. "Do you think they came to steal my raspberries?"

"Looks like they may have done that already," Concord said. "There aren't any berries here. Let's go ask them why they broke their deal."

Concord and Logan made their way up the river to the Burley twins. As soon as Concord got a close look at the twins, he started to chuckle. Bart and Bernie both had purple stains all over their faces and hands.

"Looks like you've been enjoying some raspberries," Concord said.

"Says who?" Bernie replied.

Logan giggled. "Says your face," he said.

Bart and Bernie looked at each other, then wiped off their faces.

"Well," Bart said. "I guess it was our lucky day. After we gave you that other raspberry patch, we found this one."

"You may have given that raspberry patch to me before, but it's gone now," Logan complained. "You took all my raspberries."

Bart leaned over to Bernie and whispered in his ear. Bernie nodded.

"Now, why would we do that when we have all of the raspberries we could possibly eat right here," Bernie said as he pointed behind himself.

Concord and Logan looked behind Bernie and saw a lush raspberry patch with perfectly ripe berries.

"You must have pulled my plants up and planted them over here," Logan protested.

The twins leaned toward each other again, and Bernie whispered into Bart's ear. Bart nodded and walked over to a nearby raspberry plant.

"If that was true, how could I do this?" Bart said. He grabbed the end of a raspberry vine and leaned way back on his heels. Suddenly, the vine snapped and Bart fell flat on his back.

"Ouch!" he cried.

The other three boys laughed.

"As my brother has so gracefully demonstrated," Bernie said, "these plants have been in the ground for a long time. You can see that the roots of the vine that snapped are still firmly in the ground."

Concord walked over and inspected. It was true. The roots of the plant weren't budging, so the plants couldn't have just been replanted.

"I think I heard a bear roar a little while ago," Bernie said. "It must have eaten all your raspberries. Bears love wild berries, you know." The twins chuckled.

Concord began to reach for one of the berries. Bart jumped back up to his feet and blocked Concord's hand.

"Unfortunately, Mr. Concordance," Bart said, "this patch is off limits to you and Logan." Bart pointed to a rope along the edge of the patch. "This rope marks Burley berry territory."

Concord looked down at the rope, and he noticed that Bart's feet were wet. So were Bernie's. Concord scratched his chin as his eyes flashed from the right to the left. Then he raised his head and looked at Bart.

"I think you're mistaken," Concord said. "If you're going to keep your deal with Logan, then these raspberries are his."

"Why should we give him our raspberries just because a bear took his?" Bernie questioned.

"Nice try," Concord said, "but Logan's raspberries didn't get eaten by a bear."

"Oh yeah?" Bart said. "Prove it."

"Okay," Concord replied as he unzipped his backpack.

Logan was confused. "Why are these raspberries mine, Concord?" he asked.

"We've been so concerned about the raspberries, we forgot about the real key to what happened," Concord said.

Concord pulled out his Bible and rustled through the pages as fast as the wind. He finally stopped in 1 Kings.

"Here," The Concordance said to the group. "Read 1 Kings 5:8-9. What Bart and Bernie did has been done before."

How did Concord know that the raspberry patch belonged to Logan?

Read 1 Kings 5:8-9 to find the clue Concord gave the group.

The solution to *"River Raspberries"* is on page 90.

12
THE
OUTLAW'S SHED

Mr. Cunningham had the look. He walked quickly around the house, gathering various items.

Concord watched from the couch. He had seen this many times before. His dad was just about to go on an interesting reporting assignment.

"May I come, Dad?" he asked.

Mr. Cunningham bit the side of his cheek in thought. "This one is quite a ways out of town," he said. "It's out at DeLaney's Ranch."

"The dude ranch?" Concord asked excitedly.

"That's the one," Mr. Cunningham said, putting on his jacket. "I'll be gone a few hours, so there wouldn't be much time for homework afterwards."

"That's okay, it's all done," Concord said, relieved that he had just finished.

"Okay then, partner," Mr. Cunningham said with a cowboy accent. "Let's saddle up and move 'em out."

"Yee-haw!" Concord shouted as he grabbed his jacket.

Mr. Cunningham scribbled a note for the rest of the family, and he and Concord were off. After driving about forty miles south of Pine Tops, they got to the edge of DeLaney's Dude Ranch.

Ranch guests got to experience real ranch life. They herded cattle, rode horses, and even learned to lasso.

"Is your assignment to describe what DeLaney's Ranch is like?" Concord asked.

"Nope," his dad said. "Rex DeLaney, the ranch owner,

called the paper today. He said that he just found the branding iron of Wild Bob McGraw."

"Wasn't McGraw a famous cattle rustler?" Concord asked.

"Very famous," his dad confirmed. "McGraw stole cattle from ranchers down here about eighty years ago. After he stole the cattle, he'd brand them like they were his own. His brand became famous. That's why this branding iron is such a find."

"How do those branding irons work, anyway?" Concord asked.

"They're iron rods with some kind of design fastened to the end of them," Mr. Cunningham explained. "Often the design was a shape, a letter, or a combination of the two. The ranchers would heat that end of the iron in a fire until it got red hot. Then they would press it against the cattle."

"Ouch," Concord said. "Sounds like instant hamburger."

"I'm sure it was a little painful," Mr. Cunningham said. "But it burned the rancher's design into the cattle's hides, so everyone would know who they belonged to."

"Then how could Wild Bob McGraw steal the cattle if they were already branded?" Concord asked.

"Legend has it that McGraw's branding iron was twice as big as everyone else's," Mr. Cunningham said. "It had a big solid circle in the middle of the design. McGraw would brand right over the top of the other rancher's brand."

"So the big solid circle in McGraw's brand would cover up whatever brand had been there first," Concord concluded.

"Exactly," his father said.

After driving through a big log gate, they parked next to the ranch office. It was just to the right of the corral. As soon as the Cunninghams opened their car doors, Rex DeLaney burst out of the office to meet them.

"Howdy, partners!" he hollered. He had on a large white cowboy hat and a belt buckle about as big as a small pizza pan. "You must be Mr. Cunningham from the *Ponderosa Press*."

"Nice to meet you," Mr. Cunningham said, shaking hands. "This is my son, Concord."

Mr. DeLaney pulled out an imaginary pistol and shot Concord with a wink.

"I know you city folk are always in a hurry, so let's get right to it," Mr. DeLaney said.

"Alrighty," Mr. Cunningham agreed. He pulled out his reporter's notepad. "Did you find Wild Bob McGraw's branding iron on your property?" Mr. Cunningham asked.

"Sure did, partner," Mr. DeLaney said. "It was on the eighty acres out back that I bought last month." He pointed toward the land beyond the corral. "There's a ghost town just over that hill. I was up there this morning taking some pictures of the old church when I realized that I'd never looked in the shed behind it. When I opened that shed door, I could hardly believe my eyes."

"McGraw's branding iron was in there?" Mr. Cunningham asked.

"Yessir," Mr. Delaney replied. "Can you believe it? McGraw used to hide out behind a church! Not too many folks would think to look for him there. He was a clever old rustler." Mr. Delaney shook his head and sighed. "And he was the worst outlaw these parts have ever seen."

"But isn't McGraw sort of a hero now?" Concord asked.

"Yep," Mr. DeLaney nodded. "Kind of a mixed up world, ain't it? Folks seem to take a likin' to famous outlaws for some reason. I guess that's why Billy the Kid and Jesse James are so famous. Anyway, when folks hear that my ranch was where Wild Bob McGraw did his dirty work, I think my business is going to pick up quite a bit."

"Can we see the branding iron?" Mr. Cunningham asked.

"You betcha," Mr. DeLaney said with a grin. "It's still right where I found it, and it won't take us more than two shakes of a horse's tail to ride up there in my truck."

The group hopped into Mr. DeLaney's truck and headed for the ghost town. Before long, the rustic brown church came into view, and behind it was the old shed. There was a broken lock hanging from a latch on the shed door.

"I had to bust that lock to get in," Mr. DeLaney said as the group approached the shed. "It looked like it was a hundred years old." Then he swung open the door. "Welcome to the hideout of Wild Bob McGraw, just as he left it!"

The Cunninghams walked cautiously into the shed and Mr. Delaney followed.

"There she is," Mr. DeLaney said, pointing over to a tool bench. "It's going to be a humdinger of a tourist attraction."

Concord walked over to the tool bench and looked at the branding iron. It was huge. He began to reach for it to see how heavy it was.

"Not so fast, little fella," Mr. DeLaney said. "I'm not letting anybody move that branding iron. For all we know, Wild Bob McGraw himself may have been the last one to touch it."

"So you haven't even picked it up yourself?" Mr. Cunningham asked.

"No way," Mr. DeLaney said. "This here's an authentic exhibit, just as McGraw left it."

Concord pulled his hand back. Then he studied the design at the end of the iron. There was a big circle in the middle of the design, just as his dad had described. Attached to the outside of the circle were letters that spelled out "McGraw." The design was attached to an iron rod that was about four feet long. The rod was about an inch thick and solid black.

Mr. Cunningham looked around, then turned to Mr. DeLaney. "I'm surprised this shed is still standing," he said.

"Yesiree," Mr. DeLaney said. "It's pretty run down. I'll have to patch the roof and brace the walls before the tourists start coming in. I want the place to be safe. I suppose I'll have to lock the place up at night, too."

Concord looked at the leaning walls and the shoddy roof. There were cracks and small holes everywhere due to years of neglect.

Mr. Cunningham decided he had enough information and closed his notebook.

"Looks like you've found yourself quite a treasure, Mr. DeLaney," Mr. Cunningham said.

Concord's eyes opened wide as he remembered something that the Bible said about treasures. He looked back at the branding iron. Then he turned to his dad.

"I'm afraid this is no treasure at all," Concord said.

"I don't know why not, Concord," Mr. Cunningham replied. "I think people are going to be pretty excited to see Wild Bob McGraw's branding iron."

"I'm sure they would be," Concord said. "But this can't be Wild Bob McGraw's branding iron."

Mr. DeLaney took off his cowboy hat and put his hands to his hips. "What do you mean, little fella?" he said. "It says McGraw right on it."

"I think you'd better read Matthew 6:19," The Concordance said. "There's something in there that you must have forgotten."

How did Concord know the branding iron wasn't Wild Bob McGraw's?

Read Matthew 6:19 for the clue that Concord gave Mr. DeLaney.

The solution to *"The Outlaw's Shed"* is on page 91.

Solutions

Solution to The Vase Case

Acts 9:25 tells about Saul (later known as Paul) being lowered down a city wall in a basket. The electrician got the vase out of the apartment building in the same way. He tied all of Mrs. Jessen's blankets together as a rope substitute. He then put the vase in the emptied picnic basket, unlocked the window, and lowered the basket to the alley below.

When the basket touched the ground, he went down to the alley and moved the vase from the basket to his van. He then went back up to the apartment and pulled the basket up. This is why he was seen going up to the apartment twice by the security cameras while carrying nothing. When he had pulled up the blankets and basket, he locked the window.

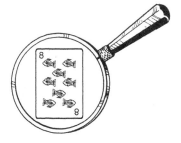

Solution to The Forehead Game

Proverbs 27:19 refers to water reflecting a man's face. Dustin was able to look down into his mug of water and see a reflection of his own face. He could then see what card he had on his forehead in the reflection. After looking at everyone else's cards, he could easily figure out how low or how high his card was.

A dark mug in particular, like Dustin's green one, allows water to give a good reflection.

Solution to Sidewalk Chalk Talk

Joshua 10: 13-14 describes a day when the sun stood still in the sky. The passage also says that such an event hasn't happened again since then. Concord realized that if the sun is always moving across the sky, the statue's shadow is always moving, too. When the Burley twins claimed it took them two hours to trace the statue's shadow, Concord knew they had to be lying. The statue's shadow would have moved too much during those two hours to be traced in one spot.

Solution to The Party Piggy Bank

Romans 9:21 indicates that a potter can make more than one item out of one lump of clay. In this case, Rodney made two piggy banks out of his lump of clay. Concord realized that Rodney's piggy bank was smaller than other students' creations because Rodney needed enough leftover clay to make a second bank. Nobody knew that Rodney had made the second bank because all the sculptures were microwaved at home.

Rodney stole the money simply by swapping the empty piggy bank for the full one. The short time during the afternoon break when Mrs. Pound and the rest of the class were out of the classroom was all the time Rodney needed to make the swap.

Solution to The Sap Whapper

Psalm 42:7 mentions the noise of a waterfall. Before Mr. Lock played the tape, he claimed that the recording was made at the base of the thirty foot-high Grand Pine River Falls. Concord realized that if Mr. Lock was next to the waterfall, the waterfall's roar should have been rather loud on the tape. But right after Mr. Lock silenced his wife on the tape, and right before the bird song was heard, the recording was silent. The lack of waterfall noise meant that Mr. Lock's tape was fake.

Fortunately, Mrs. Cunningham was able to catch President Birk right before the prize check was handed to Mr. Lock. The only birds Mr. Lock heard that night were fellow jailbirds.

Solution to The Stolen Flamingo

In Genesis 19:26, Lot's wife was turned into a pillar of salt. The White Flamingo statue was also made out of salt. When the museum's vault filled up with water, the statue dissolved. When Concord tasted the leftover water, its saltiness gave away the artist's plan.

Since the vault was sealed, the artist knew it would fill up with enough water to dissolve the statue, provided the sprinklers ran long enough. He cut the fire bell wire so people wouldn't come to the museum and turn off the sprinklers when they couldn't find a fire.

The artist made the statue appear stolen without even breaking into the museum! Rather than getting the insurance money, the artist ended up with nothing but jail time.

Solution to Redhead Rocks

1 Samuel 17:40 mentions how David pulled five "smooth" stones out of a stream. Smooth, round rocks are found where there is moving water, or where water was moving long ago. The rock that the twins gave Concord for inspection was also smooth and round. Yet, the twins claimed it came from the top of Mount Redhead. Concord realized that any rock that is actually from the top of a tall mountain like Mount Redhead wouldn't have the appearance of being eroded by running water.

The twins were forced to confess that they had spray painted rocks that were actually from the bottom of the Grand Pine River. They were stuck with a backpack full of rocks and a big paint bill.

Solution to Collapsing Crackers

Luke 6:49 refers to a torrent, or flood, washing away a house that doesn't have a good foundation. Rodney realized that a flood of water would turn a graham cracker cabin's foundation and walls to mush, which would then make the cabin collapse. To do this, Rodney came up with the perfect time-delayed sabotage: putting the ice he got for his supposedly sprained ankle into Charlotte's cracker cabin.

The ice slowly melted and soaked into the cracker walls and base. They became mush and the cabin collapsed. Since the two finalist cracker cabins were on separate tables, Rodney knew that his cabin would be safe from the melting ice. He "politely" let Charlotte put her cabin in the office first so he could sabotage it with the ice when he took his cabin into the room.

Solution to The Dawn Skimmer Challenge

James 3:4 explains that a ship is steered by a rudder. The sailboat that Mayor Ritzo constructed was made from a rowboat, which doesn't have a rudder. Instead, rowboats are steered by their oars.

The mayor only took one oar, which was being used as the mast for his sail. As a result, he had no way to steer his boat to McCall's Dock. The rules stated that the winner was the first person to tie up at McCall's Dock, so the mayor was sure to lose.

Mayor Ritzo did get across the lake slightly faster than the Dawn Skimmer canoes. However, the mayor was about a half-mile down the shore from McCall's Dock. By the time he pulled his boat to McCall's Dock, every one of the Dawn Skimmer canoes had beaten him.

Solution to Topless Trees

Psalm 11:2 describes the process of bending a bow, putting an arrow against the string, and shooting. Concord realized that Cheryl Riley was able to do the same thing when she was in Mr. Brown's tent.

Using her good arm, she bent her green walking stick into a bow and used her shoelace as a bowstring. She then pulled out the sponge that she had smuggled into the tent. She stuck the sponge on the end of a stick and dipped it into some of the red paint that was still in the tent. Then she shot the sponge like an arrow.

Though she couldn't bend her right arm because it was in a cast, she could still use her right hand to pull back the arrow. After taking several shots at the tree trunk, she took the shoelace off the walking stick. Then she walked out of the tent as if nothing had happened.

Solution to River Raspberries

1 Kings 5:8-9 tells of logs being hauled by water. The Burley twins used the river to move the logs that had marked the location of the raspberry patch.

The twins knew that Logan would use the logs as a landmark when he tried to come back to the raspberry patch. So, the twins put the logs in the water and floated them downstream a couple hundred feet.

The twins then pulled the logs onto the river bank and went back to the raspberry patch. They ate as many berries as they pleased, believing they could fool Logan into thinking that they were eating from a different patch.

They would have succeeded, had Logan not invited The Concordance along.

Solution to The Outlaw's Shed

Matthew 6:19 mentions a treasure being destroyed by rust. Concord realized that if the branding iron had really belonged to Wild Bob McGraw it would have been rusty.

The shed, with its leaky roof and walls, would have given the branding iron no protection from the weather. Iron, in particular, rusts when it is exposed to moisture and air.

Mr. Cunningham did more investigating and discovered that Mr. DeLaney had devised the branding iron scam to bring more guests to his ranch. The newspaper decided to make the attempted scam a front page story, and Mr. DeLaney had fewer guests than ever.

Concord's Secret

If your Bible has a Concordance, it will usually be found at the back of the book. It is a collection of the most common words found in the Bible, with their most used examples in the text under the word. Sometimes there is a brief description of what the word means. Learning how to use a Concordance gives a Bible scholar a marvelous tool for finding God's Truth on any subject in His Holy Word.

Below are a few examples of words found in the Concordance. Read them for practice, look up the verses, and you will see how much fun it is to do your own Scripture Sleuthing. Then get your Bible and you will be able to solve your own mysteries in life.

Appearance - brightness, radiance, sight
I Samuel 16:7, man looks at the outward *appearance*
Matthew 6:16, for they neglect their *appearance*
Matthew 28:3, his *appearance* was like lightning

Friend -
Proverbs 17:17, a *friend* loves at all times
Proverbs 18:24, a *friend* who sticks closer than a brother
John 15:13, lay down his life for his *friend(s)*

Impossible -
Matthew 19:26, with men this is *impossible*
Luke 1:37, nothing will be *impossible* with God

Money - gain
Ecclesiastes 5:10, who loves *money* will not be satisfied
Mark 6:8, no *money* in their belt
I Timothy 3:3, free from the love of *money*
Luke 19:23, why ...not put the *money*...bank

Parents -
  Matthew 10:21, children will rise up against *parents*
  Romans 1:30, disobedient to *parents*
  Ephesians 6:1, children, obey your *parents*

Sword -
  Genesis 6:24, flaming *sword* which turned
  Psalm 57:4, their tongue, a sharp *sword*
  Ephesians 6:17, the *sword* of the spirit
  Proverbs 5:4, sharp as a two-edged *sword*

Glad -
  Matthew 5:12, rejoice and be *glad*
  Proverbs 10:1, wise son makes a father *glad*
  2 Corinthians 11:19, bear with the foolish *gladly*

Serpent -
  Genesis 3:1, Now the *serpent* was more crafty
  Psalm 58:4, venom of a *serpent*
  John 3:14, Moses lifted up the *serpent* in the wilderness.
  Matthew 10:16, be shrewd as *serpents*

Trouble - distress, affliction
  I Kings 20:7, see how this man is looking for *trouble*
  Job 5:6, does *trouble* sprout from the ground?
  Psalm 9:9, a stronghold in times of *trouble*
  Proverbs 10:10, who winks the eye causes *trouble*

If you have enjoyed solving the mysteries along with Concord Cunningham, you may wish to read

The Scripture Sleuth 2:
Concord Cunningham Returns
ISBN 1-885904-25-8

The Scripture Sleuth 3:
Concord Cunningham on the Case
ISBN 1-885904-39-8

The Scripture Sleuth 4:
Concord Cunningham Coast to Coast
ISBN 1-885904-53-3

Visit the Scripture Sleuth website at
www.scripturesleuth.com

For other biblical titles from Focus Publishing visit
www.focuspublishing.com.